ONE OF THE SE
WESLEY'S ESSEX C

THE HAUNTED COLCHESTER AREA

A COLLECTION OF GHOSTLY STORIES AND MYSTERIES

WESLEY H. DOWNES

A WESLEY'S PUBLICATION

BRITISH LIBRARY CATALOGUING - IN - PUBLICATION DATA.
A CATALOGUE RECORD FOR THIS BOOK IS AVAILABLE FROM THE BRITISH LIBRARY.

£3.95

Copyright © W. H. Downes. 1992.

ISBN: 0 9519289 2 9.

All Rights Reserved
No part of this publication may be reproduced, stored in a retrieval system, or transmitted in any form without prior written permission from the publisher.

Published by Wesley's Publications, 61 Lymington Avenue, Clacton-on-Sea, Essex CO15 4QE.

First Published 1992.

Printed by Guild Press (Clacton), Clacton-on-Sea, Essex.
Typesetting: Essex Phototypesetting, Clacton-on-Sea, Essex.
Front cover design by Rose Bishop.
Drawings by Rose Bishop and Malcolm Batty.
Photograph of Chalkney Mill by D. McKenna.

AUTHOR'S ACKNOWLEDGEMENTS

I am greatly indebted to all who have contributed stories and information so freely to me, and duly acknowledge the authors of previously published works.
I also wish to thank those who have assisted generally in reading and correcting the manuscript.

INTRODUCTION

The author is hopeful that the contents of this book will provide the reader with as much pleasure as he has received in the collecting and researching of these stories.

Many have never been published before but some are classic local ghostly stories, without which the book would have been incomplete. So far as possible, the truth and facts have been strictly adhered to, but of course, there are times when a little 'poetic licence' is necessary to help the story 'flow', so I hope the reader will forgive me for any undue 'embroidery'.

Ghosts and Hauntings provide a fascinating subject for discussion, but there is one big regret — they will not appear on command. If only one could arrange for an apparition to be at a certain spot at a given time, so much of the mystery might be explained, and the cynical sceptics would be silenced for ever.

But in the meantime, one must have faith in the lucky people who happened to have been in the right place at the right time to see and/or hear various manifestations, and have been able to record their experiences.

Without such people, it would have been impossible to have collected the stories contained in this book. So to them I say a big "Thank you". I am sure that the reader will echo this sentiment.

I hope that you will not only enjoy reading this book, but want to read my other publications of similar vein.

Sleep Well.

W.H.D.

CONTENTS

HAUNTED COLCHESTER

Ardleigh	The Young Lady On The Mile Stone	Page 6
Gt Bentley	The Phantom Dog	7
Brightlingsea	A Grave Story	8
	The Motorcyclists Shock	9
	It Pays To Be Polite To Thomas	10
Colchester	The Mystery Of The Pond	11
	The Haunted Fish & Chip Shop	12
	The Phantom Eyes	13
	The Haunted Childrens Ward	14
	A Ghost Of Colchester Castle	15
	What Could The Dog See?	16
	The Haunted Red Lion	17
	A Strange Visitation In Colchester	19
	The Lost Roman 9th Legion	21
	Haunted Berechurch Hall	23
	Ghosts From The Civil War	25
	The Day When The Devil Claimed His Man	26
	The Haunted House In Abbots Road	28
	The Chattering Corpse	30
	The Strange Story Of St Leonards Church	36
	The Mystery Of Duncan's Gate	36
Copford	The Bishop's Return To Church	37
Dedham	The Haunted Sun Hotel	38
	The Baby Sitting Ghost	38
	The Wandering Ghost	38
	The Haunted Workhouse	39
	The Playful Child Ghost	39
	Memories Of A Dedham Lady	40
Earls Colne	Chalkney Mill	42
Feering	The Return Of The Old Soldier	45

Langenhoe	The Haunting Of Langenhoe Church & Rectory	47
Lawford	Lawford Church Stories	49
	The Mysterious Church Choir	50
Layer Marney	Layer Marney Towers	51
Manningtree	Manningtree Hauntings	53
Mistley	The Haunted Thorn Hotel	54
Mersea Island	The Roman Ghosts Of Mersea Island	56
	More Ghostly Footsteps	57
Tollesbury	The Ghosts Of Tollesbury	58
	Ghostly Dogs	59

OUT OF TOWN GHOST STORIES

Nayland	The Haunted White Hart Hotel	12
Harwich	The Mystery Of The Ghostly Voices From The Sea	18
Loughton	Dick Turpins Ghostly Ride	25
	Black Shuck	41
Ford End	The Black Chapel	46
	Phantom Animals	46

ARDLEIGH

THE YOUNG LADY ON THE MILE STONE

Ardleigh has a ghost of a young lady who early in the mornings likes to sit on a mile stone beside the main road.

She appears to be so realistic and solid, that one morning a farm worker saw her get up and without saying a word walked beside him as far as the nearby farm house where she walked right through the closed front door, it was only then it was realised that she was a ghost.

This young lady had been seen sitting on that mile stone many times over the years, but seldom has it been realised the she was actually a ghost.

Perhaps she once had some connection with that farmhouse!

GT. BENTLEY

THE PHANTOM DOG

There is a story of a phantom dog that has been seen many times running along the back gardens of a row of Council houses at Gt. Bentley. Many people claimed that the dog has a pheasant in its mouth, presumably the pheasant is phantom as well!!

A tenant of one of the houses laid in wait for several nights with a double barrelled 12 bore shot gun at the ready. One night his patience was rewarded. Just as it was getting dusk he saw the ghostly dog appearing through his neighbours fence, carefully taking aim, he waited until the apparition was about ten yards away, then squeezed the trigger twice — there was no way he could have missed, the hound certainly disappeared without trace.

For nearly a year nothing was seen of the phantom animal, but then one night a young boy claimed to have seen it, but this time there was no pheasant in it's mouth!!

Trying to find a possible explanation for the appearance of such an apparition is difficult, but so far there are only two possible suggestions. First probability is that the dog was part of a shooting party and went to retrieve a pheasant that had been brought down. But perhaps a novice or trigger happy "shot", saw something moving through the undergrowth and took a pot shot at it, killing the dog.

The second possibility though, suggests that a poacher took a shot at a pheasant and the dog, perhaps from a nearby cottage, saw the bird fall and ran to retrieve it. The poacher, seeing the possible loss of his quarry, took another shot and killed the dog.

BRIGHTLINGSEA

A GRAVE STORY

In Brightlingsea's churchyard there is an altar tomb near to the south door that is known as the 'atheist's' tomb. This is the tomb of John Selletto, who died in 1771. It was said that most of his life he had been a confirmed atheist and just before he died he said that if there really was a God a tree would grow from his grave.

Some years later, lo and behold, a tree did grow from the tomb. As it grew so it gradually pushed the tomb apart until it was leaning at a dangerous angle, at this point the authorities decided to take the tomb apart, remove the tree and rebuild the tomb.

Of course, over the years there has been endless speculation about this tree, some say that a seed must have been placed in the coffin at the time of burial, others say that the stone masons, knowing of the story, planted a sapling whilst they were assembling the tomb. Maybe the truth will be known one day, but there is one strange point about this story — How was it, if John Selletto was such an atheist as believed, that he was buried in the south side of the churchyard in consecrated ground and not in the unconsecrated ground on the north side??

THE MOTOR CYCLISTS SHOCK

Early one morning while on his way to work, a motorcyclist travelling from Brightlingsea to Colchester was approaching the sharp bend opposite All Saints Church, when he became aware of a large white Alsatian dog padding its way from the lane leading from Moverons.

Without hesitation, the hound continued its way right into the front wheel of the motor cycle, only to pass through it and continue its way towards Brightlingsea Hall.

The man, although severely shaken, somehow managed to stay on his bike. He came to a standstill, hardly believing what he had just seen. By now his nerve had completely gone, slowly, he turned around and went home. He was certainly in no condition to go to work that day.

Subsequently, he altered his starting time for work rather than risk a repetition of this event!

****

CHURCH BELLS

The ringing of church bells in the 14th century at the time of the Black Death was thought to help to disperse the plague.

****

The ringing of church bells at a funeral was thought to scare away the dead persons ghost.

****

There have been several instances where church bells have rung on their own accord just before a disaster.

IT PAYS TO BE POLITE TO THOMAS

An unusual story from Brightlingsea has its origins in the early 1800's.

During this period Essex and Suffolk were centres for cloth-making and this industry also brought a degree of prosperity to another local industry — copperas. Copperas stone, or pyrites of iron could be found on the beaches in considerable quantities and was for many years collected by the local people and sold to the local factories where it was used for various purposes. Some were cut up and highly polished, then used to make jewellery, others less suitable for this purpose together with the waste, were ground up and used to make ink and black dye. The dye was used for dyeing cloth and leather, also when mixed with verdegris it could be used as a cure for scab in sheep.

Brightlingsea and Walton-on-the-Naze were two of the three main centres for the copperas industries. Brightlingsea had its works at the bottom of Tower Street, and it was here that tradition has it, that one night the owner of the works fell into one of the boiling vats and died.

For years his ghost haunted the works, but was quite harmless except on one point. Before anyone went upstairs, it was necessary to shout "I'm coming up, Tom."

One adventurous or careless person omitting the warning, was flung down the stairs and sustained a broken thigh!!

In recent times it is alleged that mysterious footsteps can be heard above the line of shops at Brightlingsea's Waterside. Are these of the haunting Thomas?

COLCHESTER

THE MYSTERY OF THE POND

A man was staying with some friends for a weekend on the outskirts of Colchester. On the Sunday morning, he woke early and going to the bedroom window he looked out across the fields, where, to his surprise and horror he saw in the next field a pond with what he was sure was a woman's body floating face downwards.

He hastily dressed and rushed downstairs into the back garden, but was unable to see through the fence or able to climb over it. So he ran around to the front of the house, down the road until he found a field gate and climbing over it he ran into the field but could not see any pond.

Thinking that perhaps he had lost his sense of direction in his hurry, he went back to the house, up to his bedroom and looked out of the window again. There it was — the pond, the body just as before, making sure that he got his bearings right he set off again down the road to the gate, into the field, along the fence - - - but still no pond or body.

This time he knew there was no mistake. Here was the field he had seen from his bedroom window, but definitely no pond and certainly no woman's body.

Returning again to the house, he found that by now his hosts were up and were wondering what he had been dashing about for. When he told them what he had seen, but could not find, they told him that when they moved into the house some five years previously, an elderly neighbour mentioned that some years ago there had been a pond in the field behind their house, but when a woman was found drowned in it the farmer who owned the field had it drained and filled in.

What he must have seen was a re-enactment of the scene from years ago, but why could he only see it from the bedroom window??

THE HAUNTED FISH & CHIP SHOP

A Fish and Chip shop in Osborne Street, Colchester, has the reputation of being haunted. Although not a troublesome ghost, it is at times a little mischievous.

There was the time when the young daughter of a previous owner went upstairs to the toilet. She had not been in there many minutes before she let out an almighty scream and came rushing down again, extremely pale faced, and said that as she sat on the loo she felt a ghostly hand touching her face!

A manager and his wife both had strange experiences in this same toilet; they also heard strange tappings upon the toilet door at time when they were the only ones in the building.

An early morning cleaner was working downstairs in the shop, when suddenly she heard a noise from the floor above "as if someone had swept a pile of knives and forks across a Formica-topped table". At the time she was the only person in the building and all the exit doors were locked. When she looked upstairs all the cutlery was in its normal place and there was nothing to indicate what had caused such a loud noise!

The building is certainly very old, it still has some of the oak beams from the time when it was once a public house, and there are stories that once a tunnel ran from it's cellars to St Botolph's Priory. Knowing some of the stories of old Colchester this would appear to be quite a possibility.

****

THE HAUNTED WHITE HART HOTEL AT NAYLAND

The White Hart Hotel at Nayland, near Colchester, is reputedly haunted by the restless spirit of a woman who was killed by a soldier over two hundred years ago. She still makes her presence felt after all that time.

THE PHANTOM EYES

An unusual apparition has been seen at the bottom of Clingoe Hill, Colchester.

Long before the present dual carriageway was built a man was driving his car from Colchester towards Clacton along the old Elmstead Road, when he to his amazement saw a pair of large luminous large eyes about four feet from the road level. They passed before him in a wavy motion across the road; thinking that he was imagining the whole thing he said nothing to his passengers.

When he was half way up the hill, his mother-in-law who was sitting beside him, asked if he had seen anything unusual. Not wishing to give his thoughts away, he asked what she had in mind, she replied that she thought that she had seen a pair of eyes floating across the road.

Baffled by the occurrence, nothing more was said at the time, but several months later the driver was talking with some men and the subject came round to ghosts. The driver related the incident of the eyes and one of the men said that he had heard of a similar incident on the same spot many years ago. His grandfather had been a groom at Wivenhoe Park, (where the Essex University is now) and he had heard his grandfather relate the story of the time when there had been a big party at the Park, and when the guests were leaving quite late at night, one coach pulled by four horses was making its way along the track as it was then, down hill at quite a speed, near the bottom of the hill a herd of deer ran across in front of the coach, there was a crash and the coach turned over and although the occupants were badly shaken but otherwise unhurt, some of the deer were killed. It is thought that the phantom eyes were the wide eyes of a deer blazing with fright at the impending accident which some sixth sense had told it would result in its untimely end.

Other reports have mentioned that about the turn of the century the ghostly form of a complete deer had been seen about the same area, but as time passed the body has faded away.

****

THE HAUNTED CHILDRENS WARD

There is a story that the children's ward in Colchester's Essex County Hospital was haunted by a kindly nun who dished out toffees to the children.

This story was related by a Colchester man who recalled the time when he was in this ward as a patient when he was a boy.

He clearly remembers lying in a bed, when a nun dressed in a black habit approached his bed and gave him a toffee from a brown paper bag, spoke a few soft words to him and proceeded down the ward.

As he chewed the toffee, he watched her slowly walking away, and was then astonished to see her suddenly disappear.

He is now in his fifties but the whole incident has remained clearly in his mind ever since.

A GHOST OF COLCHESTER CASTLE

When only a mere twenty years of age, James Parnell was doomed to become the first Quaker martyr when he died, a prisoner in Colchester Castle in May 1656.

Over the years many people have met an untimely death in and around Colchester Castle, some famous, such as Sir George Lisle and Sir Charles Lucas, others, like James Parnell, not so well known until after their death.

Physically weak and small in stature, he was derisively dubbed at school as the "Quaking boy," having been converted to Quakerism after visiting that famous Quaker, George Fox.

Parnell, then moved into Essex where he started preaching his beliefs and generally upsetting other religious groups. He was arrested and sent to Colchester Castle where he was held, until a few weeks later he was chained to a number of other prisoners and marched the twenty-two miles to Chelmsford for trial. He was convicted and fined £40 for "contempt of authorities". Unable to pay the fine, he was returned to Colchester Castle.

Because of the trouble he had caused the authorities, he was confined in a deep hole in the castle wall. To make life even more difficult for him, he had to climb a rope suspended from the twelve foot high ceiling in order to get his meagre allowance of food.

One day he fell from this rope and sustained injuries from which he later died, most likely through lack of medical attention.

As time passed, stories started circulating of a small, thin ghostly figure appearing through a wall in one of the lower dungeons of the castle, sometimes seeming to limp, other times just drifting across or along the narrow passage towards the spiral stone stairway. Could this be the ghost of James Parnell still making his protest??

WHAT COULD THE DOG SEE ?

Quite recently a man was walking along the Harwich Road at Parsons Heath when he saw coming towards him a man who he had not seen for some time.

When they drew close he spoke to the approaching man saying how nice it was to see him after all this time, but the man carried on walking as if he had not seen or heard him.

Not wanting to be put off like this, he turned and called after the man, thinking that perhaps the man was so deep in thought that he was completely oblivious of all around him, but on calling out his name the figure just disappeared.

When he arrived home he was still baffled by his unexpected experience, and was even more surprised when his pet dog growled, and then flew at him and bit his arm. Normally the dog was very docile and never growled let alone bite anyone.

For the next few days the man felt the presence of the man who had disappeared around him, although he did not see him again the dog however continued to growl and bark at him and generally treat him as if he were a stranger.

Could this be a case of a spirit taking possession of a body? Could the dog see the entity as well as his master and realise that something was wrong??

****

HALLOWE'EN NIGHT LEGEND

About a century ago it was an Essex belief that if one stood by the church door at midnight on Hallowe'ens night it was possible to see the shadowy figures of those doomed to die in the parish during the next year

THE HAUNTED RED LION

Colchester's oldest Hotel, The Red Lion, is said to be haunted by the ghost of Alice Miller, who, it was reported to have been "fouly done to death" in 1633. She is said to haunt the hallways and stairways of the hotel.

On occasions, chambermaids have reported having heard their names whispered whilst working in the bedrooms and assuming they are being called by a colleague, have turned round, only to find that there was nobody there.

Several of the staff have said that at times they have felt that there is a presence watching them at work, also a certain coldness has been felt in the corridors, but rarely has anyone reported actually seeing anything.

In 1972 considerable building works were being carried out when the builders stumbled across a sealed off section which obviously had once been a part of a room. This was almost certainly the legendary 'haunted room' which for years the hotel staff had been forbidden to talk about, even amongst themselves, in case it might affect any nervous guests.

Legend has it that several hundred years ago "something horrible" happened in that room. Exactly what it was has long been forgotten and all record of any occurrence has been destroyed 'for the good of the business'.

However, whatever caused the room to be haunted, the result was that as word got around guests staying in the hotel became terrified and soon left, and trade was badly affected.

The then owners of the Red Lion, or perhaps at that time it might have still been known by its old name — The White Lion, decided to close the older part of the building 'for renovations'. By the time that section was refurbished and re-opened, thanks to the silence of the staff, the legend was soon forgotten and trade picked up.

Whether the "something horrible" was to do with the death of Alice Miller and her being "fouly done to death" is not certain, but the date 1633 suggests that it could well be so.

Although there are no recent reports of anything untoward happening, there are certain parts of this rambling old hotel that some staff are hesitant to answer 'room service' calls late at night!!

****

OUT OF TOWN GHOSTS

HARWICH

THE MYSTERY OF THE GHOSTLY VOICES FROM THE SEA

Many times over the years from the early 1800's, people walking along the promenade near to the Redoubt, on the sort of day when a sea mist rolls in from the sandbanks that abound around this part of the coast, voices have been heard across the water, not just ordinary voices, but hoarse, rugged voices, speaking in old fashioned nautical terms — "Eight by the mark," "Six by the mark," "Long shore ahead," etc. etc.

Knowing how voices can travel across water under these conditions, it is impossible to say just from how far away they appear to originate. They could be close to the shore, or could be as far out as the sandbanks, also, as there is no sound of engines, it is reasonable to assume that the voices come either from a sailing boat or perhaps from a boat propelled by oars.

There does not appear to be any record of a wreck with the loss of life near to the Redoubt, so the mystery goes on, who were these ancient mariners? Why should these voices still be heard?? Maybe one day all will be revealed.

A STRANGE VISITATION IN COLCHESTER

This is a strange story that defies explanation; perhaps it is a time warp of some sort, even a weird figment of a man's vivid imagination, possibly the real answer will never be known, but one thing is for sure - the young man who actually saw the incidents will swear that it is all true and nothing will persuade him otherwise.

In 1974 four young men from Colchester set off by car to travel to Manchester to support Ipswich Town Football Club against Manchester United.

Half way along the motorway they stopped at Keele Service Area for a break. Having refreshed themselves, two of them returned to their car, the other two went to the toilet. Whilst there, one of them suddenly noticed the figure of a man standing beside him dressed in old fashioned clothes similar to those of the civil war period. (1640) The figure was wearing a wide brimmed hat, a broad white collar and roughly woven light brown clothes which had a form of very coarse stitching holding them together.

Thinking that the figure was that of a man taking part in some type of war games, or possibly a publicity stunt, even an actor engaged on a film set, apart from an odd glance as the man left, he paid no more attention to him.

Rejoining his friends in the car, they continued their journey. As they travelled along he asked the others what they thought the man might have been doing, but to his surprise none of them had even seen the figure, even though it was so conspicuous. The matter was dropped and conversation returned to the forthcoming match.

Nothing more was thought of the incident and the months slipped by until one day the young man, who by now had married and was living with his wife and mother-in-law in East Street, Colchester, was idly standing looking out of his front room window at the old Siege House Restaurant opposite, when to his utter amazement he saw a figure walking along the pavement opposite dressed exactly as he had seen the man in the Keele toilet over a hundred miles away.

The figure with his strange form of dress strolled along, but the other pedestrians didn't even seem to notice him, nobody even gave him a second look, it was uncanny.

At first he couldn't believe his eyes, but yes, the figure was definitely there, he called out to his wife and her mother to come quickly. He pointed out the figure to them, but his wife said that she could not see anything unusual where he was pointing, but her mother was able to describe exactly what the man was wearing, even saying when the figure turned the corner towards the rear of the Siege House to disappear from sight.

The Siege House, now a restaurant, is an old timbered building that takes its name from the famous siege of Colchester in 1648, in fact it has a number of musket bullet holes in its timbers that were fired during the siege and these holes can still be seen today.

But the mystery of the figure remains unsolved!!

THE LOST ROMAN 9TH LEGION

In the late 1880's, farmers used to employ boys for the pricely sum of one penny a week to scare the rooks and pigeons away from their crops. For this princely sum they were expected to walk up and down the fields shouting and clapping two pieces of wood together from early morning to sunset.

In the hot, dry summers of that period it was no wonder that by midday the boys became very tired and would often find a shady spot near the hedge to have a quiet snooze.

It was under these conditions that one such lad succumbed and having found a nice spot under a large oak tree, sat down. Within a matter of minutes he was fast asleep. Some time later he was awakened by the sound of marching feet in the dusty lane on the other side of the hedge.

Running to the field gate, he was astounded to see hundreds of soldiers marching along at a fast pace and he then realised that they were all dressed in a strange uniform with helmets and swords and between each section was a standard bearer. After what seemed an age, they disappeared in the distance into a cloud of dust.

The rest of the day dragged badly for the boy, he was just aching to get home to tell his parents and friends what he had seen. After all, it was not every day that one saw columns of soldiers, especially what he now thought to be Romans.

That night he found the energy to run home and excitedly he related his story, but to his dismay nobody would believe him. Nobody else had seen any soldiers, let alone Roman and anyway there had been no Romans in this country for hundreds of years, so the boy must have been dreaming.

Word got around about the boy's 'dream' and a good laugh was had by all. Sometime later however, a schoolmaster heard of the story and remembered being taught in a history lesson, that when the Romans were in occupation of this country, there was a time when the 9th. Legion consisting of some three thousand men, left their quarters in the north of England to march to London by way of York, Newmarket, St Albans and possibly Colchester.

After leaving their far north camp, nothing whatsoever was heard of them again; over three thousand men just disappeared off the face of the earth. It has been suggested that they might have been ambushed and all killed, but if this had been the case, word would have got around about it and also there would have been some evidence of a battle. After all, these were well trained soldiers, probably the best in the world.

The mystery was never solved it seems to have been an early 'Bermuda Triangle' type of disappearance.

Coming back to the boy's experience. Could he possibly have seen the ghosts of this missing Legion still marching on towards Colchester and London, after all, the spot where the boy claimed to have seen them would have been very close to the route that the Romans might have taken!

What the boy saw could very well have been a re-enactment triggered by some time warp.

The boys story was related by his great grandson, who stated that to his dying day his great grandfather swore that he really did see that Roman army!!

HAUNTED BERECHURCH HALL

Berechurch Hall was demolished in 1953, but long before that, it had the reputation of being haunted by the ghost of a 'Lady in White'.

This 'Lady in White' is said to be the ghost of Charlotte White, who was one of the Smyth family who lived at the Hall for many years.

The story that has been related many times over the years, is that Charlotte played 'fast and loose' behind her husbands back. Eventually of course he found out what had been happening, but because his love for her was so great, he forgave her.

It would appear that her conscience troubled her so much that even when she died, her restless spirit came back to haunt the old Hall.

During the Second World War the Hall was occupied by the military. There is a story that a soldier on guard fainted one night. When he recovered, all that he could say was " I saw a ghost, a lady dressed in white!" Apparently he tried to stand his ground, until, she almost walked through him, then he just passed out!!

A caretaker also said he saw a female figure dressed in white, slowly walking along a path at the rear of the house, and also, what was believed to be the same figure gliding along a corridor and yet another time, it was seen coming out of one of the bedrooms.

Other ghosts were believed to frequent Berechurch Hall. The shadowy figure of a man was seen one night on the landing, also the library door has been known to open and close on its own volition, and door handles have also rattled at odd times. Footsteps have been heard even during the daytime let alone at night along the corridors and stairways.

Since the Hall was demolished, there have been no reports of any 'sightings', but perhaps now that the site has been built over, Charlotte and her friends are more settled.

When eventually the Hall was demolished, it was revealed that many years ago, a curse was put upon anyone removing one of the oak wall panels!!

It is also believed that a monastic building stood on the site long before the Hall was built and that a tunnel used to go from the building to the old St John's Abbey, but that perhaps, is part of another story.

****

CHURCHYARD WATCHERS

In days gone by when villages were growing and new churches were being built it became necessary to have new graveyards .

It became a superstition that the spirit of the first person to be buried in a new graveyard was supposed to stand guard over the graves, this spirit became known as the Churchyard Watcher, he or she was skull-headed and wore a white or grey shroud.

This was one of the ancient pagan beliefs which survived in remote parts of the country, including Essex.

GHOSTS FROM THE CIVIL WAR

Although the siege of Colchester was in 1648, there are still stories of the ghosts of some of its gallant defenders still carrying out their duties.

A fine example of loyalty can be found in Colchester's Headgate Court, where there have been reports of a ghostly cavalier who has been seen and more often heard still carrying out his guard duties around the grounds on windless nights.

Another old house in Crouch Street still has the ghost of a Royalist drummer boy, the roll from his phantom drum is not heard quite so much nowadays, but occasionally his fading figure can be seen leaving the building at dusk.

****

OUT OF TOWN GHOSTS

DICK TURPINS GHOSTLY RIDE

Not too far away from Dick Turpin's hideout in Epping Forest there was an old widow, a Mrs Shelley, who lived in a cottage on Traps Hill, Loughton.

Old Mrs Shelley was said to have her life savings hidden away somewhere in the cottage and in due course Dick Turpin got to hear of this. With some of his gang he decided to help the poor old lady spend the money; so one night they forced their way into her cottage and demanded the money. When she refused to tell them where it was hidden they got hold of her and roasted her over her own kitchen fire until, screaming with pain, she eventually told them.

Having found the money they left her on the floor to die in agony from her extensive burns.

It is said that anyone walking down Traps Hill late at night could well encounter the sight of Dick Turpin on a phantom horse riding like the wind with the ghost of old Mrs Shelley, her scrawny fingers round his neck and her face all twisted and distorted with fear, pain and hatred for her cruel murderer.

THE DAY WHEN THE DEVIL CLAIMED HIS MAN

This very strange story was related by a Colchester man who's mother actually had the experience when, in the early 1930's she was about eight years old.

Sometime before the Second World War was even thought about, Stanwell Street, Colchester, was well known as a rather run down area. Most of its two down, two up cottages were without bathrooms, and the toilets, such as they were, sometimes crudely known as 'thunder boxes', were outside, sometimes at the bottom of the small yard and even this description has not done them any injustice!

However, it was living under these poor conditions, with low wages, and cheap beer, that drove many of the male members of the family into the Robin Hood public house on the corner to drown their sorrows and to try to escape from reality, even if only for a short time in an alcoholic haze.

In those days, Sunday mornings would see these men waiting outside the pub for opening time at twelve o'clock, then they would spend the next two hours putting the world to rights. This was of course, unless some harried housewife decided to literally enter man's domain, and drag her husband home before the Sunday dinner was altogether ruined.

Such was the situation that this story is based upon, but, in this instance, instead of the wife going for her man, the young eight year old girl was sent to get her father.

She ran from the scullery, down the back garden path, through the broken paled gate that led into a narrow alley.

Reaching Stanwell Street, she found herself face to face with a strange thing, the like of which she had never seen before — it was an animal form, with a body of a fat Alsatian dog, but the head of a goat with horns!

She stopped dead with fright, the creature seeming quite oblivious of her, waddled its way towards the Robin Hood. The girl, as soon as she regained her senses, turned around and ran back to tell her mother what she had just seen.

Her mothers prompt reaction was to say "Oh My God, it's the Devil, he's come for your father!" With that, she dropped the tea towel that she had in her hands and ran as fast as she could to the pub.

Reaching the door, she was aware of an uproar within, voices were raised and the whole place was in a state of turmoil, everybody seemed to be shouting at once and it was obvious that something very unusual had happened.

Pushing her way through to the bar, she demanded to know not only where her husband was as she could not see him, but also what was all the trouble in the pub?

The harassed barman said that as far as he knew her husband had gone outside to the toilet, and the 'trouble' was, one of the customers had a fit and had jumped up screaming "No, No, not me". Then he had fallen down dead!!

****

GHOULS

The term 'ghoul' is applied to a revolting form of Demon, found in Asia, which feeds on corpses.

A version of 'ghoul' is used in this country to describe a feeling of horror and oppression which is often accompanied by a sensation of intense cold, this is not regarded as being a ghost — a ghost is regarded as being a visible or partly visible thing.

THE HAUNTED HOUSE IN ABBOTS ROAD

There is a house in Abbots Road, Colchester, that was built before the turn of the century on the site of a former Rectory. So far as can be ascertained, there is no logical reason for the present building to be haunted, but, as in the best of traditions, houses that have been built on the sites of old rectories should be haunted, so why break with tradition ?

The present occupiers have lived there for a number of years, but during this last eight or so years, various things have happened that makes them believe that the place is also occupied by the spirit of a young girl, who at times makes her presence felt in many ways.

Items are often moved from one place to another, sometimes even disappearing for days, then re-appearing either in the place from where they were removed, or in an entirely different location.

One Christmas a large bow was purchased to be placed upon the Xmas tree, but it strangely disappeared, only to re-appear some days later in the bathroom!

That same Christmas, some parcels placed under the Xmas tree, disappeared, but were later found upstairs in a bedroom !

On another occasion a room mysteriously filled with smoke for no apparent reason, it hung about for some time, then disappeared as quickly as it had appeared!

There was a time when an air refresher flew from the downstairs toilet, across a passage, into the kitchen. It did not hit anyone, but there was a 'near miss'; before it then fell gently to the floor!

Another time, the lady's sister had been staying in the house for a few days with her two year old daughter. Just before they were about to leave, and were standing in the kitchen, a film cassette was thrown from where it was placed on the window sill, across the room at head height, just missing the sister, to crash into the door. It was thought that this was done to show the spirits annoyance at the little girl leaving!

The reason that it is thought that the spirit is that of a young girl, is because it is always brightly coloured things that are moved or perhaps played with !

One time when their seventeen year old son was in a room, the bookcase doors opened and a book fell, landing on the floor open at a page on which there was a poem that had been discussed only a few days earlier!!

Strange footsteps have been heard in various parts of the house, but when the house has been searched, nothing or anybody that could have caused them could be been found!

Although most of the 'happenings' could really be described as mischievous, there was one time when it is thought that the spirit world saved them a great loss.

The house had been burgled, drawers ransacked, and valuable items stolen. In one of the drawers there had been a small cardboard box that had contained a gold chain; the box had been broken open and the contents removed, presumed stolen.

A few days later, when the drawer was opened, the lady was surprised to find that the box was restored almost to its former condition and the gold chain was inside it!! Yet the police had seen the box in its damaged condition, and there was definitely no chain to be seen anywhere. Had the spirit been aware of what was about to happen and decided to remove the chain first ??

These are mysteries that may have never been solved, but in the meantime they certainly give food for thought!!

THE CHATTERING CORPSE

A LEGEND OF ST. JOHNS ABBEY

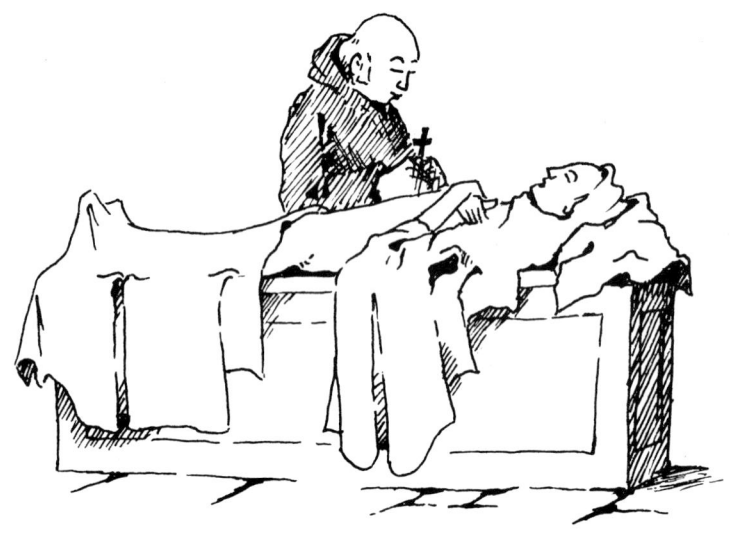

Shortly before Christmas of one of the years towards the end of the thirteenth century, there was quite an unusual incident at St John's Abbey, Colchester.

Although a cold north-easterly wind swept the snow in drifts against the Abbey walls, inside, it was warm and quiet. Travellers who were spending the night at the Abbey were sound asleep on their straw mattresses, St. John's being well known to regular travellers as a place where they could be sure of a good meal and a night's rest.

Just before midnight, a bell rang denoting that somebody was at the wicket gate wishing to be let in, the duty monk gathering his gown and a lanthorn went to see who it could be at this time of night.

When he reached the gate, he asked who was there. A feeble voice replied "A poor wayfarer who seeks shelter for the night". "Brother, you are rather late", said the monk as he opened the gate. "Yes, I am; I lost my way and had to follow the town wall until I found a gate into town". The monk then led the traveller to a room where there was a fire to warm him and went to fetch him a bowl of hot soup.

By the lantern light, the traveller's face showed long furrows in his cheeks and the wrinkles on his brow seemed to tell, not of age, but of long suffering, his clothes, bearing and speech made it clear that he belonged to a class much higher than the ordinary peasant.

After the meal, the monk showed the old man to his cubicle where a bed of a pallet of straw was made as comfortable as possible.

During the night the old traveller was taken ill and by the next morning was unable to leave his bed. The Sub Prior was called and he immediately sent for the Chirurgeon who, after bleeding him, shook a doubtful head as to his possible recovery.

As his condition continued to deteriorate, Father Osmund — the Sub Prior — offered to shrive him, but the old wayfarer said that he had confessed a week previous and had been absolved, but in any case he hoped to recover and continue his journey.

Two days passed, but the wayfarer's condition failed to improve, when suddenly there was a turn for the worse and the Sub Prior was called once again to give the last rites of the Church.

"Have you confessed all? Is there no secret sin that you have not confessed ?" said Father Osmund. But there was no answer. "If you cannot speak, raise your finger in token, that I may grant absolution". Slowly the finger was raised, so solemnly absolution was pronounced, but the last rite was hardly finished when the old man gasped, shook, then laid still. His soul having departed, his body was left as a pale, emaciated corpse.

The passing of the old man seemed to have a strange effect upon Father Osmund, who had not always been a monk. In his younger days he had been a Colchester Burgher of considerable means, but after some domestic trouble — the deaths not only of his wife but also his son, he gave all his property to the Abbey as was the custom of the time and became a monk and with time, rose to the rank of Sub Prior.

When Father Osmund had gathered himself together, he ordered that the corpse should be taken on a bier to the mortuary and placed in front of the small altar. Candles were lit at the head and foot and the passing bell to be tolled at the twelfth hour. Two monks were to keep watch until the funeral could take place after Christmas.

It was just 24 hours after the wayfarer's death that screams came from the mortuary cell. They came from the two monks who had been standing vigil. The screams were followed by the two monks themselves who rushed from the mortuary shouting "Horrible! Horrible! Horrible!"

This aroused the other monks who came to see what the noise was about, but all they could get from the frightened watchers was "Horrible, Horrible!"

When, a few minutes later the Sub Prior appeared and demanded to know what the commotion was all about, one of the watching monks just managed to stammer "Go not there, stay, stay, the corpse is chattering". To demonstrate this, he raised his head, chattered his teeth and rolled his eyes. "It was horrible, just horrible". He then explained that they were kneeling and praying when the corpse moved, raised its head and chattered with its teeth.

"If this is so" said the Sub Prior, "the poor fellow could not have been dead, but only in a stupor". "Nay! Nay!" they replied, "He is certainly dead".

At this, Father Osmund decided to go to the mortuary cell himself, but, not surprisingly, no one followed him. However, being a pious man, he did not fear the supernatural and felt that whatever he found, God would protect him from any harm.

On reaching the cell, he found all was quiet; the corpse was lying still, the candles burned without a flicker and everything had an air of a deathly stillness. Looking at the corpse, he could not understand what had frightened the two watchers, so he decided to lift one of the eyelids to see if there was any sign of life in the corpses eyes, but just as his fingers touched the corpses face he saw a movement from the cold clammy body. At this he stepped back and repressed a startled cry. The eyes and mouth opened, the corpses teeth started to chatter.

At this, the startled Father stuttered "In the name of the Three Persons of the Blessed Trinity are you the Fiend that disturbs the rest of the dead ?" To which the corpse replied, "I am no fiend; I am the man who died yesterday. This is my corpse, Holy Father. Will you listen?"

Frightened and pale, the good Father braced himself to listen, then the teeth chattered again and the voice said "Alas! Father, yesterday when dying I told you I had confessed all my sins. That was a lie told with dying lips, for I hoped to hide my wickedness in the grave. I had confessed all my sins — but one — one great crime. This I hoped to hide — no one knew it but myself and God. Alas! Alas! The agony I have suffered!"

After a brief silence the corpse continued "My soul went up, but they would not let me in . I would go to purgatory for a thousand, nay a million years and purge myself — but no — it could not be". "Go back", an Angel cried to me in a voice of thunder, "go back to earth and confess to Father Osmund, for the unconfessed and unshrived dead shall not enter here". "So here I am back; will you please hear my confession?"

At this Father Osmund looked at the now silent corpse and faintly whispered "Yes".

Then the corpse said "It is a long story, but it is a truly awful one. I am a murderer of the worst sort. I was a native of this town and was brought up of a God-fearing family. When I was a young man, I courted the daughter of a yeoman here. I had a rival, who eventually won her hand in marriage, so, to cure my passion for revenge, I left this town and wandered over Europe".

"After ten years, I came back a changed and sobered man. I found that during my absence my old sweetheart had died leaving a son who was now seven years old. Fate brought me into contact with the lad and I loved him as though he were my own child. It was then that I entered this very Abbey as a monk and for two years I lived a peaceful life — until one day — the blackest day of my life".

"The lad and I, who were now great friends, meeting regularly and often went on walks together. His father, who was now a substantial burgess of this town, little dreamed that this monk with whom his son went fishing was his old rival in love".

"On this black and awful morning the lad and I went to the town pond to fish. Alas! how many times have I wished that I could blot out that fateful day in my life. Having rowed our punt to the middle of this large deep pond we had started fishing when the lad accidently fell overboard. For a moment I was paralysed, then I reached over and caught hold of him and I could have easily saved him but instead of pulling the lad into the punt, the sudden desire of revenge on his father overcame me. I held him under the water and although he struggled desperately, I continued to hold him under until he finally drowned".

"Then I rowed to the side of the pond and disappeared until a few days ago. But his face has haunted me day and night and has finally driven me here to die".

"What happened to the lad's father I never did find out, but oh, how I suffered for my crime and now I am not to be allowed even into Purgatory until I have confessed here, — near the very spot where the crime was committed".

With this startling confession over, the chattering teeth were still. Father Osmund stood frozen to the spot. Not a word had he uttered during this sad, sad story, but his thoughts weighed heavily.

"Father, I crave absolution, may I not have it?" chattered the corpse once again. "Do you truly and sincerely repent of this terrible crime?" asked the monk. "Yes, Yes" said the corpse, eagerly, "Every day I have repented, in fact every hour for over twenty years, indeed I have suffered and I cannot face that voice up there without your absolution. Can I please have it, for I long to be at rest?"

"Brother" said the Sub Prior slowly, yet firmly, "I too have suffered terribly for more than twenty years, it was I who was your rival!! The boy that you murdered was my only son, my greatest treasure. I always thought that he was drowned by accident and submitted myself to the will of the Holy One. I gave up everything and came here. Little did I think that I was the victim of a cruel and revengeful rival".

Although it did not move, the corpse appeared to be listening until again it chattered "Father, Father, I repent! I confess! Your injury is greater than my crime. Can I please, please, obtain absolution?"

"Brother" said Father Osmund solemnly, "For this terrible crime, repented for years and only confessed after all worldly things are over, God may forgive you. I cannot!!".

As soon as these words had been spoken, the corpse issued an unearthly cry that seemed to shake the whole building. The yellow teeth chattered, the staring eyes rolled, the whole body shook. Then all was quiet.

Father Osmund stood for a few minutes looking down at the grim spectacle, then overcome with his own intense emotion, collapsed.

After the corpse's final cry, the monks who until now had kept their distance from the cell, summoned up their courage and picked up the trembling body of their Sub Prior and took him back to the refectory.

When Father Osmund had recovered sufficiently, he nevertheless felt unable to tell his Brothers anything of what had happened in the mortuary cell, but when the Abbot — who had been away from the Priory all this time — returned, he was told the whole story by Father Osmund.

After listening in silence, the Abbot, with a gentle reprimand, said "Brother, think you not that you should have given this poor sinner absolution?"

But Father Osmund answered "No, I could not. My humanity stood aghast at the heinousness of the crime. A million years of penance can never wipe it out. Let him stay in Purgatory for ever".

"Alas" said the Abbot, "This poor unhappy being was turned away from eternal happiness until he had confessed to you and had received your blessing. Now that he has confessed, he still has not obtained your forgiveness and blessing. Indeed Brother, this must weigh heavily in your heart".

At this rebuke, Father Osmund feeling the effects of this eventful last few days suddenly clutched at his heart, collapsed and died.

No sooner had the body of the unfortunate Sub Prior touched the floor, than there was a terrible scream from the body of the corpse in the mortuary. The monks all took this to be the final scream from a departing spirit condemned to spend an eternity in Pergatory.

THE STRANGE STORY OF ST LEONARD'S CHURCH

If only it could talk, the old, now disused, St Leonard's church on Colchester's Hythe Hill, could certainly tell some strange tales. However, as it can't, we shall just have to recall but one of its stories that have survived the course of time.

With its old oak hammerbeam roof and the carved rood over the chancel entrance, alas, only five now remain of the original twelve carved wooden figures ornamenting the wooden roof.

A curious story associated with these wooden heads goes back into the dim and distant past, when four of the heads used to peer through the iron bars in the chamber above the church porch. Legend has it, that these were the heads of four robbers who were condemned to starve to death for attempting to rob the church. Having compassion, a passing baker threw them a loaf of bread, but he was seen to do this and was duly arrested and condemned to suffer the same fate with them. Could it be that the five remaining heads represent these five men?

When walking on the opposite side of the road to the church, it is said that if you cast an eye up to the window over the porch, on occasions, the ghosts of the four robbers can be seen looking out.

****

THE MYSTERY OF DUNCAN'S GATE

Many times when people have passed by Duncan's Gate at Colchester Castle they have remarked of suddenly feeling cold, depressed and aware of a sensation of some prevailing evil.

A Spiritualist medium who was not even aware of the name of the gate, thought that she picked up some connection with Scottish soldiers and also felt that there was history attached to the nearby mound, but because of the number of people in the vicinity she could not pick up anything more specific.

COPFORD

THE BISHOP'S RETURN TO CHURCH

Copford's St. Mary's Church is reputed to be haunted by the ghost of the infamous Bishop Bonner who was rector of this church for many years and was buried under the high altar in 1569. His apparition has been seen several times over the 400 plus years since his death, even in recent years.

It has been reported that his ghost has been seen standing at the altar, dressed in full ecclesiastical clothes and holding his staff. Then he silently and slowly descends the altar steps before disappearing.

At other times, he has been seen and heard walking up the pulpit steps, thump the pulpit top, followed by a noise like a heavy bible being closed sharply, shortly to be accompanied by footsteps descending the pulpit, then walking the full length of the nave to disappear through an old church door that had been locked and bolted for years, followed by the sound of a door being slammed.

One day the church organ was being tuned. The tuner, accompanied by a lad who was sitting at the organ with a pile of books stacked beside him. They had been laughing and joking about the bishop haunting the church — when all of a sudden, the pile of books were swept to the ground, just as if they had been pushed by some unseen hand!!!

DEDHAM

Dedham, once regarded as a small town, was also one of the first places in Essex to have its own gas works and gas street lighting. It owed its past prosperity to the wool industry which also helped to provide Dedham's magnificent church.

Dedham Vale was immortalised by local artist John Constable and the area soon became known throughout the world as Constable Country.

As with most long established villages and small towns, Dedham is reputed to have it's fair share of ghosts and hauntings as the following selection will show

THE HAUNTED SUN HOTEL

The Sun Hotel at Dedham is said to be haunted by the ghost of a serving wench whose remains were supposed to have been buried in the garden at the rear of the hotel after being burnt as a witch, her misty form is supposed to appear when there is going to be a disaster.

THE BABY SITTING GHOST

There is an old house in Dedham's High Street that has a gentle ghost who's aim in after life seems to be caring for young children when they are in their bedroom. The children often ask "Who was the man watching us last night?" A figure appears by their bed and stands there sometimes smiling, sometimes just looking and then glides slowly towards the front of the house and disappears close to the wall. The children are so used to seeing him that they show no fear, in fact they look forward to his visits.

Perhaps it could be the apparition of an old family servant still carrying out his earthly duties which he might have enjoyed doing!

THE WANDERING GHOST

Dedham has another well known female ghost that has been seen many times. She glides across the cricket field behind the Church, seeming to come from the grounds of a large house adjoining the sports field. Her grey wispy figure then turns into a lane before entering an old barn in the adjoining football field.

It has never been established just why she should make this walk nor the connection with the barn!

THE HAUNTED WORKHOUSE

The old Dedham workhouse was said to be haunted until about 1976/7. It was about this time when the building was being converted into a house that the builder, having realised that there was a 'presence' there, brought in a Spiritualist medium to carry out an exorcism.

His reason for taking this action was not because he thought that the 'disturbances' would have proved detrimental to the sale of the building, but to finally put this earthbound spirit to rest.

The treatment seems to have been successful, as there have been no recent reports of any further manifestations.

THE PLAYFUL CHILD GHOST

There is a cottage in Bargate Lane, Dedham, which is said to be haunted by a ghost of a child, who still likes playing with earthly toys.

Many times the children's toys have been seen to move around on their own volition, and when the family is away from the cottage for the day it is not unusual to return to find toys scattered around the place just as if someone has been playing with them in the family's absence!

So far there have been no reports of the ghostly child having been seen, although there is often a strong 'feeling' of another child or children being in the house!

MEMORIES OF A DEDHAM LADY

A lady who spent her younger days in a 400 year old Dedham cottage, told of some of the ghostly scenes that she had witnessed there in the days when she was a young girl and on into her late 'teens.

She recalled that the first apparition that she saw was that of "a tall figure in a long dark cloak and a flat brimmed hat"; the figure had appeared outside a window.

"I watched the unusual scuttling movement of his feet as he passed and re-passed the window." "He did not give the impression of being a solid human being and yet, not what I had been led to expect of a ghost. His face was very pale, with no real features or expression."

It was rather strange, but most of the 'sightings' were seen through this one window. She saw the shadowy figure of an old man in a long dark coat. Not only did he have a pronounced stoop, but the most disturbing thing was, that where his face should have been, there was just a grey void.

There was the time when she was amazed to see what appeared to be the figure of a lady friend of hers. What really amazed her was, she knew that her friend was alive and well, and that day was visiting a relative some miles away.

The figure she had been watching was an exact 'double' of her friend, but her actions were rather strange. Every movement she made, appeared to be rather exaggerated, also she seemed to repeat her actions two or three times. There was just no explanation for this at all.

Although as stated, all these unexplained 'sightings' were seen from this one window, there was one incident that took place outside in the garden.

By this time, she was in her late 'teens and as it was a lovely summers day she was walking round the quite large garden. She had just come to the fair sized brick shed which many years previously had been a combined wash-house cum bakehouse, when she saw a tall middle-aged, very well dressed lady who, to all intents and purposes was a normal live human being also taking a walk in the garden. However, our lady was so surprised to see somebody that she gave a startled cry, and the figure just disappeared!!

Despite several attempts to find answers, no possible explanations have been found for any of these strange apparitions, nor for the mystery of that one window!

****

GHOSTLY DOGS

BLACK SHUCK

Black Shuck is said to be a devil dog, that roams the coastal lanes all along the East Anglian coast, from Norfolk down to Essex.

It is said to be the earth-bound spirit of excommunicated 12th century villain Hugh Bigod.

He takes the form of a large black dog, sometimes with a single blazing red eye in the centre of its forehead, sometimes as a headless animal with a pair of red blazing eyes protruding just about where its eyes would have been, other times with eyes said to be as big as saucers.

It pounds its way along along the lonely windswept coastal lanes on stormy nights, and woe betide the unwary traveller that suddenly comes face to face with it, for legend has it that to do so, it is a harbinger of death and disaster, especially for the beholder.

EARLS COLNE

CHALKNEY MILL

Chalkney Mill is situated on the boundaries of Earls Colne and White Colne. Actually the boundary is defined by the River Colne and as the river flows through the middle of the old mill, half of it is in Earls Colne and half in Great Tey.

Dating back to the 16th century the mill was an undershot fulling watermill, but time has taken its toll. The old water wheel has long since disappeared but the building has now been restored into a very comfortable family home with several unusual features, after all, how many houses are there with a river and a waterfall in the centre of the lounge, also a giant horizontal gear wheel complete with its old oak drive shaft?

In 1865 the mill was enlarged to twice its present size, and although long since reduced to that of today, it is still large enough to have six good size bedrooms and a lounge well over 20ft long, with room to spare for more rooms if ever they should be required.

Carved on one of the old oak beams is the name William Dell. 1811. and the same name is also etched on a brick near a staircase. Whoever William Dell was is not known, perhaps he was a miller at the time.

The family of the present owner have lived in the adjoining mill house since the 1930's, the mill then being worked by the father until his death.

Whilst the mill was being converted into a dwelling house, although nothing was actually seen, the workmen on several occasions heard unaccountable noises and footsteps. Once they clearly heard copper piping being moved about in a room below where nobody was working, when they looked, there was no one there and the copper piping was still in a bundle lying on the floor!

The adjoining mill house was built on the site of a former 15th century cottage and dairy, and at times the strong aroma of moss roses can be smelt when moving through the house into where the dairy building once stood.

Shortly after the occupier moved in, his wife clearly saw the figure of an old lady standing at the kitchen door, but when she called out to her, the figure just disappeared!

A teenage daughter said that she was often aware of a presence in her bedroom and had once seen a dim shape there, also she heard the sound of heavy snoring in her room.

An aunt of the young lady said that some years ago she saw the figure of a man in one of the bedrooms; he was dressed in old fashioned riding habit and just stood there staring until he just faded away!

The owner of the mill house used to have a white cat which had a habit of being able to open the back door by jumping up and pressing down on the latch. Several times since its death they have witnessed the ghost of the cat jumping up and the door would swing open just as it did when the cat was alive. Three of the family related this story without being aware the others had already said the same thing.

Just behind the mill and mill house there is a large area of very old woodland with a path leading through it towards Great Tey.

Three of the family relate that at different times when walking in the woods, they have seen a phantom dog, possibly a Corgi or a dog of similar size. Other people have also seen this dog many times.

Sounds of a galloping horse have been heard travelling along the path through the woods and on one occasion a lady stood back close to a tree when she heard the sound of hooves. Fully expecting the horse to pass her, but as the sounds became level with her all she felt was the rush of air, but no horse or rider.

Another lady, however, did see the ghostly horse and rider who appeared to be dressed in old fashioned clothes, she also heard the sound of the horses hooves and the heavy breathing coming from the horse!!

Although there is no suggestion that there is any connection with the above story, it is said that King Harold hunted in these woods, also that the Black Prince hunted there when he stayed at Wakes Colne Hall.

There is an old record that Earl De La Warr was ordered to hunt and destroy the wild pigs that roamed in these and nearby woods as they were causing a great deal of damage in and around Earls Colne.

****

ROMAN MILES

The Romans introduced milestones to England, but they used to measure Roman miles, which were based upon one thousand military paces, - milia passuum. It has always been known that the Romans marched everywhere with a long steady stride that they could keep up for hours on end.

The Roman mile when measured, proved to be 1620 yards, whereas our present day mile is 1760 yards, but maybe it is only a question of time before we change to kilometres.

FEERING

THE RETURN OF THE OLD SOLDIER

A strange story from the not so distant past (the late 1890's) recalls the experience of a vicar whilst visiting Feering.

The Rev. Armisted Faulkner was touring Essex visiting sites where John Constable found inspiration for his famous paintings. He duly arrived at Feering church.

Having spent some time admiring the Tudor brickwork from the outside, he went inside to view the interior splendour. As was customary for a visiting cleric, he sat down in a pew to offer a prayer.

When he had finished, he raised his head and looked around the church to get his bearings and his eyes were drawn to a figure of a man leaning against the wall near to the pulpit. The figure was in ragged clothing and was clutching its side as if in agony. Although the light inside the church was poor, he could clearly see that the man appeared to be bleeding profusely from a wound in his side.

Rev Faulkner called out to the man and made his way towards him through the pews. In his hurry, he tripped over a hassock on the floor and fell flat on his face. Momentary stunned, he picked himself up and carried on towards the wounded man, but to his amazement the figure had gone.

Thinking that the man had run away whilst he was on the floor, the vicar went outside in case the wounded man had collapsed through the loss of blood, but there was no sign of him.

Walking away from the church Rev Faulkner saw a man cutting a hedge. He approached him and asked if he had seen the wounded man pass that way. The hedgecutter looked at him for a few moments and then said "I don't want to upset you vicar, but it's John Hardman you be looking for. There's a snag though, John's dead. He was killed some years ago in the Zulu War in Africa. He's buried over there". Pointing in the direction of a grave. "He's not been seen this last few years — he used to come quite regular, his poor side bleeding and all!"

OUT OF TOWN GHOSTS

FORD END

THE BLACK CHAPEL

Although Ford End is not strictly in the Colchester area there are a couple of rather unusual ghostly stories that it is felt will never-the-less be of interest.

Each year hundreds of visitors flock to Ford End's 500 year old Black Chapel to see its tiny altar and miniature baptismal font, also secretly hoping to see a ghostly wedding party.

A few years ago a group of visitors were just about to leave the Chapel when they were amazed to see a number of horse drawn carriages coming towards them. As the carriages neared, it became obvious that they were part of a wedding party with everyone dressed in Victorian style clothes.

The visitors, enjoying this unexpected spectacle prepared to take photographs as the carriages pulled to a halt outside the Chapel, but suddenly the whole illusion disappeared!!

One lady who witnessed the whole scene was left in such a state of collapse that she had to be given medical attention.

Just why such an incident should have taken place at all is a mystery in itself, because there are no records of any marriages ever taking place at the Black Chapel!!

THE PHANTOM ANIMALS OF FORD END

Ford End is also reputed to have two ghostly animals to its credit — One is the apparition of a white horse that manifests around the Rolphy Green area so suddenly that it scares the living daylights out of anyone who sees it, and the other is a headless cow that materialises, where else — Cowcross Lane!!

LANGENHOE

THE HAUNTING OF LANGENHOE CHURCH AND RECTORY

The old church of Langenhoe dated back to the 14th century and although most of it was destroyed in the great 1884 earthquake it was rebuilt, but eventually it became so unsafe that in 1962 it had to be pulled down.

Over the years there have been several reports of hauntings and to say the least, 'unusual happenings', both within the church and its adjoining churchyard also at the nearby old manor house which also served as a Rectory.

Apart from psychic phenomena, this church has seen drama as well. It was within these walls that Lady Felicity was murdered in the 15th century.

In 1937, Rev. Ernest Merryweather came to Langenhoe, but before he retired some 21 years later he related just a few of the 'unusual and mysterious' incidents that he had witnessed himself during his years at the church.

One day he was walking through the church when the statue of St. George coughed as he passed, he could hardly bring himself to believe that a statue could cough, so he rushed back into the churchyard, but there was nobody in sight, the statue had really coughed!!

There was another occasion when he heard the sound of an old man coughing. He was standing in the church looking up at the roof, when he clearly heard a cough behind him, the sound appeared to come from within the wall where there was an old bricked up doorway which used to be the 'private' entrance used by the lord of the manor and his family.

Then there was the time when he was standing by the belfry wall, he heard a female voice say "You're a cruel man". He turned around just in time to see his pocket knife that he kept in his pocket, being thrown to the floor with the large blade opened. There was no sign of anyone else in the church. He later found out that a murder had been committed on that spot.

Other strange things have happened; a woman has been heard singing, in French inside the church even when the building had been locked up for some time.

Then there was the time about 1949 when Rev. Merryweather was holding a Holy Communion service. His attention was drawn to a figure of a woman aged about thirty years, dressed in a long white dress with a flowing headdress. She moved across the church to disappear through the wall where some seventy years earlier there had to been a door — the same bricked up doorway where he had previously heard the coughing!

The church bells have tolled by themselves several times, even though the church was securely locked, apparitions have been seen on many occasions and several people have heard and seen things that cannot be accounted for.

In 1950, the church was filled with the strong aroma of violets, but strangely violets were not in their flowering season and in those days perfumed aerosols were not freely available, so it could not have been anyone playing a prank.

The B.B.C. sent a recording team in 1961 to try to record some of the happenings, and earlier the Society of Psychical Research carried out an investigation here.

As if all that happened within the church and the churchyard was not enough trauma for the Rev Merryweather, he was again troubled in the Rectory. The female figure that he had seen in the church manifested again in the Rectory on more than one occasion.

Then there was the time when lying in bed just dozing he was suddenly aware that he was not alone. He found himself being embraced by a naked female who he was unable to see, but felt her bare body and breasts being presssed against him, and her soft arms feeling their way round him!!

One wonders if this female could have been the Lady Felicity who was murdered in the church. Why was she murdered, and by whom?? Maybe one day further research will reveal all!

LAWFORD CHURCH STORIES

There are two stories associated with Lawford church — both are connected with brides.

There is a photograph in existence showing a wedding group standing outside Lawford Church having their photographs taken after the ceremony. The bride and groom are standing in the customary centre positions, everybody putting on their best and biggest smiles, then click, the perfect photograph to remind them one day of this the happiest day of their lives. That was what was intended, but when the photograph was developed, it clearly showed the bride being pushed to one side and another girl taking her place with the bridegroom.

How this could happen is a mystery, nobody recognised the girl and the bridegroom swore that he had never seen her before.

****

Another unusual story which was first told some years after the last story, which may or may not have any connection.

A phantom bride has been seen many times running from the church door, through the churchyard, along the footpath towards Manningtree station, her wedding-dress flowing in the wind.

Who this young bride was remains a mystery, no one can ever recall a bride leaving her bridegroom stranded at the church.

****

There is a story of a ghostly male form that rises from one of the graves in a corner of the graveyard and then glides across the churchyard, along a public footpath towards Manningtree!

The grave concerned dates about 1894.

****

There is a strange legend, that if one carries out the right procedure at a certain grave in the churchyard, it is possible to call up the Devil. To do this one has to say the right incantations whilst dancing 'widdershins' (anticlockwise) around the grave.

THE MYSTERIOUS CHURCH CHOIR

The time was 1940 — wartime. As was happening all over the country — a young lady had been to the railway station to wave good-bye to her soldier boyfriend after spending a far too short a leave at home.

After the train had left, the young lady who came from the village of Lawford, started on her way home. By now it was after ten thirty at night, but although dark, the moon was shining enough for her to see her way clearly along the footpath across the fields. She had no fears of taking this short cut home despite the fact that the path went through the churchyard and past the church that had a reputation for its 'strange happenings'.

As she approached the church, she was suddenly aware that the church was fully lit, just as if all the electric lights had been switched on. Bearing in mind that there was a war on and there was a very strict blackout in force, she thought that the caretaker must have forgotten to put up the blackout shutters. As she got nearer to the church, she was amazed to hear a full choir heartily singing, despite the fact that she was certain that the local choir had been disbanded 'for the duration'. Yet here was a fully lit church with a choir singing at eleven o'clock at night. Something was definitely wrong, so she went along the path to the South door of the church and tried the handle, but found that it was locked. Suddenly she became aware that the singing had stopped and the lights were no longer alight. She waited for a few minutes expecting people to come out, but when nobody appeared she became frightened and ran home.

The next day she went back to the church and saw the caretaker. After she had related her experiences to him, he said that there was definitely no lights showing in the church that night, in any case there was no electricity connected to the church and regarding the choir — there had not been a choir here since the outbreak of the war!!

LAYER MARNEY TOWERS

The tower is said to be haunted by the ghost of Lord Marney, who died in 1523 before he finished building the towers.

It is said that several times Henry, the first Lord Marney has been seen, dressed in full armour, mounted on a charger, riding down all ninety-six stairs of the 16th century Towers spiral staircase.

Apart from the spectral riding down the stairs, Sir Henry as he was, has also made his presence known many times in Layer Marney church.

There was the time in 1900, when one Helen Shaftesbury who was interested in the St Christopher paintings in Essex churches, came to see and sketch the painting in Layer Marney church. She was sitting down sketching, when she distinctly heard a rustling sound behind her, then she heard a voice softly say "Marney", looking around there was nobody there. A few minutes later she again heard the rustling followed again by "Marney". This time she got up and walked around the church, but she was quite alone, not a soul in sight.

About ten minutes later the same thing happened again, jumping up she shouted out "Who's there? What do you want?" But again there was no response. Her attention was suddenly drawn to a monument bearing the inscription 'SIR HENRY, FIRST LORD MARNEY'.

Later, she sought out the vicar and related her strange experience to him. He replied that several of his parishioners had also heard a voice calling out "Marney", but on most occasions it had been around the anniversary of Sir Henry's death, at Easter or early May. Strangely, every time the voice had been heard, someone had been looking at the St Christopher picture!!

The vicar also told Helen Shaftesbury that his predecessor had actually seen Sir Henry's wraith walking down the chancel away from the picture, and he also knew of two people who had also seen and heard the ghost, but this was at Layer Marney Towers.

In the early 1800's two workmen were engaged in carrying out repairs in the top room of one of the towers, when they heard a door keep slamming, when they found the only door that it could have been, they saw that the door was bolted and the the lock and hinges were so badly rusted that there was no way it could have been opened, let alone slam.

The same men also saw the figure of a man in armour standing by that door and around his shoulders was a cloak and in his hand he carried a large seal.

Later the men were shown the Marney Tombs in Layer Marney church and they thought that the figure that they had seen strongly resembled the recumbent figure on one of the tombs!

MANNINGTREE HAUNTINGS

THE VISITING GHOST

There is a house in South Street, Manningtree, where a ghost is said to walk through the front door, down the hallway, then goes out through the back door.

Nobody seems to know who the ghost was, or why it should always take this route, but it has been doing it for years.

THE LOST SPIRIT

The Red Lion public house in South Street, Manningtree, was said to have a jovial looking ghost, who often used to appear dressed in Victorian style clothes. He appeared to be quite a friendly type and was given the nickname of George, but sadly George has left the Red Lion for spirits elsewhere, he was exorcised.

An ex-landlady said that she always had a feeling that there was a 'something' in the club room of the Red Lion. After she had lived there for two years she eventually actually saw George and although startled, she felt he was not something to be afraid of. Wasn't it a shame that he had to go.

MATTHEW HOPKINS GHOST

Matthew Hopkins, the infamous 'Witchfinder General' used to meet some of his informants at the Red Lion and White Hart public houses at Manningtree, both of which he used as a form of headquarters together with the Thorn Hotel at Mistley.

It is said that his ghostly figure has been seen in all three pubs many times over the years.

THE LOST SEA CAPTAIN

There is supposed to be an 18th century ghost of a Sea Captain who walks along the top of South Hill, possibly making his way back to his boat.

MISTLEY

THE HAUNTED THORN HOTEL

This very old coaching Inn has seen life-and-death in many shapes and forms. It was built as an Hostelry with a range of stables which were entered through a high arch, just beyond which, there was a projecting beam with a hook in it through which a rope passed to remove the luggage carried on the top of the coaches. It is said that this was also used to hoist up drunks and minor wrong doers, with a warning that the next time the rope could well be around their necks.

Legend has it that two boys were fighting in the stables when one of them fell under a horse which kicked him on the head, resulting in his death. It is said that his ghost has been seen in and around the stable block many times over the years.

There is also said to be a ghost of a female seen and felt many, many times in the passage from the bar to the kitchen and also in the passage leading from the bar to the first floor.

A former landlord stated that when he came down in the mornings he often found various items scattered about the floor, items which had previously been on the shelves or tables. He also recalled the morning when he found that a clock and ornaments on the sideboard had all been turned to face the opposite way to which they had been the night before.

On another occasion some of the staff were sitting in the kitchen having a coffee when they heard a noise in a passage. A lady went to the door to see what had caused the noise when she saw what she described as a 'sheet of white' disappearing through some curtains.

There was another occasion when that same lady was cashing up the takings. She had the coins stacked up in piles along the counter, when the telephone rang and she went to answer it. She returned to find the coins scattered over the floor, but not one was missing.

More recently, a cleaner was hoovering a bedroom when the machine suddenly stopped. She went over to the switch on the wall in the same room and was surprised to find that the switch was already switched off, yet there was nobody else in the room and the door had been shut all the time.

The cleaners sister who also worked in the Thorn Hotel, was in the lounge bar when all the bottles on a shelf were suddenly swept to one side and crashed to the floor, although the shelf remained solidly fixed.

A regular customer of the bar who lives in the cottages opposite says that late one night in 1935 he heard a person pass through a bead curtain in the bar, but when he looked, there was nothing to be seen , but the curtains definitely parted and swung back, just as if somebody had walked through them.

Around about 1973, a young man who was living in one of the attic rooms was entertaining his girl friend one evening. He had been sitting in his usual armchair, but when he got up to go into another room, his girl friend was horrified to see yet another figure still sitting in that same armchair!

****

MORE GHOSTLY DOGS

PHANTOM MISTLEY DOGS

A spectral hound has been seen padding its way along The Walls at Mistley only to disappear when it seems to run out of road.

THE MISTLEY WHITE DOG

There is a story of a ghostly white dog runnning down the hill near Mistley station. Legend has it, that when it is seen it should be taken as a foreboding of a death to a certain family.

THE ROMAN GHOSTS OF MERSEA ISLAND

Mersea Island stands just a few miles from Colchester and is joined to the mainland by a concrete causeway known as The Strood.

At the time of the Roman occupation of Britain, Mersea was one of their fortified outposts and when the Romans left the area, everyone thought that would be the last they would hear of them. Not so. Even today, some hundreds of years later, their presence can still be heard and seen at times, albeit in a ghostly form.

The most widely known of their apparitions is the figure of a Centurion, seen and heard many, many times over the years, marching along with his measured stride from East Mersea direction, over The Strood, steadily pacing along the road towards Peldon.

Many people have seen it, including one motorist who had a fright one foggy night when he nearly ran into the figure. Two naval ratings had a similar experience but were unable to avoid running into it before being able to stop their car. They were quite shocked, even more so when they realised that there had been no bump, and on searching around, there was no body either!

Pedestrians and cyclists have also heard the steady sound of footsteps along that road, sometimes accompanied by a metalic clanking as of armour and at other times a full view of a Roman has been seen.

There have also been reports of other Roman manifestations on the Island. Sometimes a figure is seen standing on the East Mersea

Road later to be joined by two more Romans. After a little while they all fade away and this is followed by sounds of raised voices as if in an argument, then the noise of swords clashing followed by cries of pain, then all goes quiet. So far there have been no reports of anyone actually seeing the fight, just the sounds.

In the area of Barrow Hill, sounds of heavy wheels and horses have been heard for generations past.

West Mersea Hall was built on the site of an old Roman Villa and this could account for the ghostly peals of laughter from an unseen lady, who, legend has it, was a weekend visitor to the Villa accompanied by Claudius. On one of these occasions she went for a midnight swim and was drowned; her happy laughter can still be heard at various times.

A retired schoolmaster is said to have been travelling along the road with a car full of children, when a spectral Roman chariot and horses appeared in front of him.

One night a brave young man decided to camp out alone on one of the nearby islands across the marshes. It was a clear, still, moonlight night and apart from the occasional cry of a bird all was quiet and peaceful, until in the middle of the night the lad was woken by the sounds of the measured footsteps and a metalic clank of the legendry ghostly Roman soldiers gradually coming towards him. Scrambling out of the tent he was unable to see the cause of the noise, although the sound of the footsteps appeared to pass right through the tent to slowly disappear into the distance!

MORE GHOSTLY FOOTSTEPS

There is a story of ghostly footsteps, that can be heard crossing the bedroom floor of a cottage in The Lane, one of the oldest parts of Mersea. They are said to be those of an old rector who lived there many hundreds of years ago, who it was said murdered his wastrel son, then hanged himself in remorse.

TOLLESBURY

THE GHOSTS OF TOLLESBURY

Tollesbury is blessed or cursed, which ever way one looks at it, with several ghosts and hauntings.

There is supposed to be the ghost of a White Lady who is said to walk along the road near to the entrance to Gorwell Hall, legend has it that it was here that she met her untimely death by having her throat cut.

The Monk's House is also reputed to be haunted, supposedly there was another house built earlier upon this site, so it is difficult to say which one the ghost is associated with. Legend has it that there is an old tunnel which runs from the house to the Church, so maybe there is some connection here.

Some years ago there was an old Workhouse at Tollesbury, which consisted of a row of weatherboarded cottages, these have long since been pulled down, but before this they seemed to be 'home' to a particularly malevolent poltergeist, who's favourite trick was, apart from throwing things about, an apparent delight in smashing crockery.

Now that these cottages have been pulled down, one wonders where this poltergeist has gone and what it does for it's party tricks where ever it may be.

Another story relates, that many times the ghost of a white rabbit has been seen in the churchyard. Legend has it, to see a white rabbit running loose and wild is the fore bearer of news of a forthcoming death. So what does a ghost of a white rabbit foretell?

EVEN MORE GHOSTLY DOGS

Several places in East Anglia can boast to having phantom dogs, many appearing to be larger than life, often black with large red glowing eyes, although some have legends of dogs with one or sometimes three glowing eyes.

These ghostly dogs are seen pounding along lonely country lanes and tracks and some legends have it, that to see such a phantom means a death will occur in the family, and to look one of them straight in the face foretells your own death.

PELDON TO TOLLESHUNT DARCY

One of these ghostly dogs has been seen on a number of occasions running along the lonely coastal road which leads from Peldon to Tolleshunt D'Arcy.

TOLLESHUNT DARCY TO TOLLESBURY

There is quite a possibility that the above story relates to the same dog as they are basically from the same area and cover the same time span.

One night in the 1920's a young lady was cycling alone from Tolleshunt D'Arcy towards Tollesbury, a distance of only two miles, the night was cold, frosty and with the moon as bright as day.

She had just passed the lane which leads to Gorwell Hall, at a spot known as Jordan Green, where it is said that a man was buried with a stake through his heart, when she saw a huge black dog running along beside her, so close in fact that she could have touched it. It was bigger than a Great Dane and she was afraid that it would knock her off her cycle. It kept its position for over half a mile and then disappeared as quickly as it appeared.

On her return journey about half an hour later, all went well until she came to the spot where she first saw the hound. There it was again, but this time laying full length across the road, its eyes were closed as if it were asleep, and its great red tongue hanging out of its mouth. She rode quickly and quietly past it and didn't stop until she reached home.

If you have enjoyed reading THE HAUNTED COLCHESTER AREA, have you also read its companion book HAUNTED CLACTON, now available from most book shops or direct from Wesley's Publications. 61 Lymington Avenue, Clacton-on-Sea. CO15 4QE. Price £3.95 post free.

Shortly to be published

Treasure Holt — Its Ghosts, Mysteries & Stories.

Clacton Area — Mysteries, Murders and More Ghosts.

Colchester Area — Mysteries, Murders and More Ghosts.

ETC. ETC. ETC.

The publishers would welcome any stories or experiences of Ghosts and Hauntings in Essex for future books.